| DATE DUE | | | |
|---|---|---|---|
| | | | |
| | | | |
| | | | |
| | | | |
| | | | |
| | | | |
| | | | |
| | | | |
| | | | |
| | | | |
| | | | |

E
SLA

**3003400080166V**
Slangerup, Erik Jon.

**Monsterlicious**

**ARLENE WELCH ELEMENTARY SCHOOL**

# Monsterlicious

By Erik Jon Slangerup
Illustrated by John Sandford

For my son Landon, who makes life sweeter.
—EJS

For my friend Lane Ann!
—JS

The artist would like to thank Mr. Isaac Zenz and Mr. Robert Schaeffer for their patient help in the making of this book. Eleanor Sandford's scholarship in the area of monsterological taxonomy provided valuable research for this book: thank you.

Columbus, Ohio

## Mc Graw Hill Children's Publishing

Text © 2003 Erik Jon Slangerup
Illustrations © 2003 McGraw-Hill Children's Publishing

This edition published in the United States of America in 2003 by
Gingham Dog Press
an imprint of McGraw-Hill Children's Publishing,
a Division of The McGraw-Hill Companies
8787 Orion Place
Columbus, Ohio 43240-4027

www.MHkids.com

Printed in the United States of America.

1-57768-421-4

Library of Congress Cataloging-in-Publication Data is on file with the publisher.

1 2 3 4 5 6 7 8 9 10 PHXBK 09 08 07 06 05 04 03

The McGraw-Hill Companies

Bingle Bangdoodle came from a long, long line of very famous chefs. For years and years, every one of the Bangdoodles made delicious dishes in the Bangdoodle Restaurant—everyone except Bingle. He was a little different. Bingle only knew how to make one thing . . .

a disaster.

This made Bingle's father—one of the very famous chefs—a nervous and unhappy person. He was especially nervous and unhappy about leaving his son in charge of the Bangdoodle Restaurant for three whole days.

But the chef had no other choice. He needed a vacation from everything—especially from Bingle.

"Bingle," his father said one day, "I am a nervous and unhappy person, and I need a vacation. Since I can't find anyone else to put in charge, you're the chef for three whole days. Try not to destroy everything." Then he let out a great sigh, shook his head from side to side, and went off.

Bingle quickly became as nervous and unhappy as his father. He knew the Bangdoodle Restaurant was doomed in his hands.

Less than an hour passed before two snooty, snobby couples arrived for dinner, pressed and polished from head to toe. After he took their order, Bingle anxiously raced around the kitchen preparing the food and making a few mistakes along the way, of course. He dropped the noodles on the floor, burned the roast, confused the soap with the cheese, and dropped a shoe in the soup.

Meanwhile, the fancy couples grew impatient. Not sure what else to do, Bingle carried his disasters out to the guests.

"I, um, hope you like it," he whispered. Then he
scurried back into the kitchen and waited.

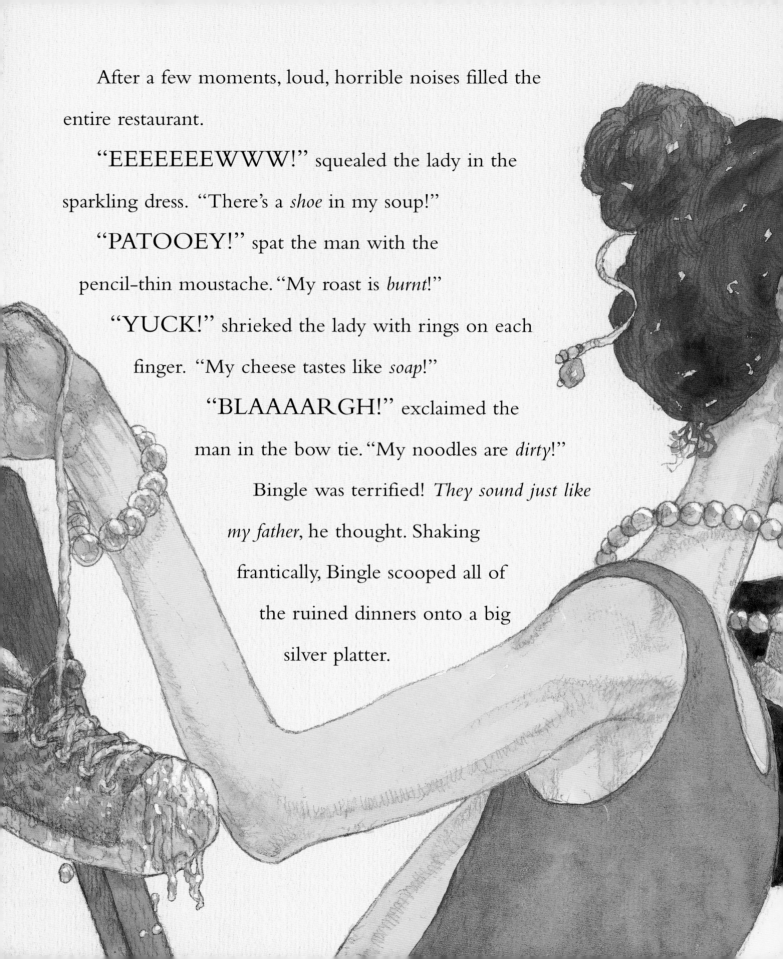

After a few moments, loud, horrible noises filled the
entire restaurant.

"EEEEEEWWW!" squealed the lady in the
sparkling dress. "There's a *shoe* in my soup!"

"PATOOEY!" spat the man with the
pencil-thin moustache. "My roast is *burnt!*"

"YUCK!" shrieked the lady with rings on each
finger. "My cheese tastes like *soap!*"

"BLAAAARGH!" exclaimed the
man in the bow tie. "My noodles are *dirty!*"

Bingle was terrified! *They sound just like
my father*, he thought. Shaking
frantically, Bingle scooped all of
the ruined dinners onto a big
silver platter.

At that very moment, something unexpected happened.

Four enormous trolls barged through the front door.

**"WE ARE STARVING!"** the trolls roared.

**"FEED US NOW!"** When trolls are starving, they are

not polite.

The fancy guests shrieked and ran, leaving Bingle
alone with the trolls. The Bangdoodle Restaurant had
never served trolls before. But before Bingle could stop
them, the trolls stomped in, squatted down at a table,
snatched the very same food off the silver platter, and
began to gobble it up.

"GOBBLEDY-GULP!" said the first.

"MUNCH-MUNCH!" said the second.

"SMACKETY-SLURP!" said the third.

"CRUNCH-CRUNCH!" said the fourth.

Suddenly, the trolls stopped eating.

Bingle stood absolutely still, frozen by fear.

"DEEEEEEEEEEEEEEEEELICIOUS!" the trolls wailed in unison.

"This shoe is scrumptious!" said the first.

"The noodles have such flavor!" said the second.

"My roast is so crispy!" said the third.

"M'mmmm, do I detect a hint of suds? How divine!" said the fourth.

The trolls all burped in unison—URRRP—so loudly that it echoed throughout the restaurant. They cheered for Bingle and congratulated him on his cooking skills. Bingle couldn't believe his ears. Never before had he received such compliments.

"MORE!" the trolls demanded.

Well, this was something Bingle could do! No longer nervous or unhappy, he busied himself by making one disgusting concoction after another. It was easy. It was fun. And the trolls loved it all!

They swallowed the soggy snake-gut sandwiches.

They inhaled the hideous hog's hair soufflés.

They munched the meadow-muck muffins.

Six hours and nineteen courses later, an exhausted Bingle worried that his guests would never leave. The trolls ate and ate and ate.

They snacked on the sticky spiderweb casserole.

They gobbled the greasy goat-gristle cobbler.

They even ate the bat-booger pie!

Eventually, the trolls called all their frightening friends
to join them. Soon, the entire dining room was filled with
monstrous beasts. Never before had the Bangdoodle
Restaurant seen such hustle or bustle.

A table of ogres dined on a plate of fungus-stuffed
frog's eyes. In the corner booth, two goblins toasted glasses
brimming with dripping dog drool. A family of swamp
creatures enjoyed slippery fish heads on a stick. And a lone
gargoyle slurped mud-puddle pudding.

By the second day, there was a long line of monsters waiting to eat at Bangdoodle's. A steady scent of old garbage wafted from the kitchen. The menu

included several daily specials: cream of cockroach, tossed worm salad, and roasted skunk on a bed of ragweed.

By the third day, the restaurant had become a celebrity hangout. Every famous creature was there. Bigfoot and the Swamp Monster were snarfing up deep-fried lint balls. Even the Boogie Man was lurking nearby. Bingle worked around the clock, while the trolls and all their friends ate everything in sight—even a candle or two.

It seemed none of the monsters would ever leave. In the dining room, they banged on the tables. They chanted for more. Bingle had never been so exhausted or so happy in all his life. He worked furiously to prepare dishes with special ingredients, like rotten banana peels, poison ivy, broken eggshells, and curdled cream. Then he remembered. Three days had passed! His father would return any moment! *What would he do?* he wondered frantically.

No sooner had this worry entered his mind than the door opened, and his father appeared. For an instant, time seemed to stop.

"BINGLE BANGDOODLE!" his father boomed. He glanced at the slime-covered kitchen walls. He glanced at the room full of hairy, bumpy, scaly guests. Finally, he glanced at Bingle, who was stirring a big pot of underwear stew. "What are you doing?"

"I'm cooking today's special," squeaked Bingle. "It's my own recipe."

Bingle's father grabbed the spoon. He scooped up some soup and sipped. Then he "hmmphed" and "hmmed."

Bingle held his breath as his father's face slowly changed from a scowl to almost a smile. Then his father did something remarkable—he winked!

"Something is missing," said Bingle's father as he stirred the soup.

Then he leaned his head back . . .

and spit out his chewing gum, which flew high into the air

and landed *ker-plop* . . . *right in the middle of the pot!*

Then, for the first time since Bingle could remember,

his father cracked a smile.

"There," Bingle's father said. "Now it's perfect."